W9-APK-828

The
Book Thing

BIBLIOMYSTERY SERIES

The Book Thing

By
Laura Lippman

Mysterious Bookshop

New York

The Book Thing
by Laura Lippman

Copyright © 2012

All rights reserved. Permission to reprint,
in whole or in part,
Should be addressed to:
Otto Penzler
The Mysterious Bookshop
58 Warren Street
New York, N.Y. 10007
Ottopenzler@mysteriousbookshop.com

ISBN (978-1-61316-044-2) (Paperback)
ISBN (978-1-61316-045-9) (Limited Edition)

The
Book Thing

*T*ESS MONAGHAN wanted to love the funky little children's bookshop that had opened just two years ago among the used bookstores that lined Twenty-Fifth Street in North Baltimore. There was so much to admire about it—the brightly painted miniature rockers and chairs on the converted sun porch, the mynah bird who said "Hi, Hon!" and "Hark, who goes there!" and—best of all—"Nevermore."

She coveted the huge Arnold Lobel poster opposite the front door, the one that showed a bearded man-beast happily ensconced in a tiny cottage that was being overtaken by ramshackle towers of books. She appreciated the fact that ancillary merchandise was truly a sideline here; this shop's business was books, with only a few stuffed animals and Fancy Nancy boas thrown into the mix. Tess was grateful that gift-wrapping was free year-round and that the store did out-of-print book searches. She couldn't wait until her own two-year-old daughter, Carla Scout, was old enough to sit quietly through the Saturday story hour, although Tess was beginning to fear that might not be until Carla Scout was a freshman in college. Most of all, she admired the counterintuitive decision to open a bookstore when so many people seemed to assume that books were doomed.

She just thought it would be nice if the owner of The Children's Bookstore actually *liked* children.

"Be careful," the raven-haired owner growled on this unseasonably chilly October day as Carla Scout did her Frankenstein stagger toward a low shelf of picture books. To be fair, Carla Scout's hands weren't exactly clean, as mother and daughter had just indulged in one of mother's favorite vices, dark chocolate peanut clusters from Eddie's grocery. Tess swooped in with a napkin and smiled apologetically at the owner.

"Sorry," she said. "She loves books to pieces. Literally, sometimes."

"Do you need help?" the owner asked, as

if she had never seen Tess before. Tess's credit card begged to differ.

"Oh . . . no, we're looking for a birthday gift, but I have some ideas. My aunt was a children's librarian with the city school system."

Tess did not add that her aunt ran her own bookstore in another part of town and would happily order any book that Tess needed—at cost. But Tess wanted this bookstore, so much closer to her own neighborhood, to thrive. She wanted all local businesses to thrive, but it was a tricky principle to live by, as most principles were. At night, her daughter asleep, the house quiet, she couldn't help it if her mouse clicked its way to online sellers who made everything so easy. Could she?

"You're one of those, I suppose," the woman said.

"One of—?"

The owner pointed to the iPad sticking out of Tess's tote. "Oh . . . no. I mean, sure, I buy some digital books, mainly things I don't care about owning, but I use the reading app on this primarily for big documents. My work involves a lot of paper and it's great to be able to import the documents and carry them with me—"

3

The owner rolled her eyes. "Sure." She pushed through the flowery chintz curtains that screened her work area from the store and retreated as if she found Tess too tiresome to talk to.

Sorry, mouthed the store's only employee, a young woman with bright red hair, multiple piercings and a tattoo of what appeared to be Jemima Puddleduck on her upper left arm.

The owner swished back through the curtains, purse under her arm. "I'm going for coffee, Mona, then to the bank." Tess waited to see if she boarded a bicycle, possibly one with a basket for errant nipping dogs. But she walked down Twenty-Fifth Street, head down against the gusty wind.

"She's having a rough time," said the girl with the duck tattoo. Mona, the owner had called her. "You can imagine. And the thing that drives her mad are the people who come in with digital readers—no offense—just to pick her brain and then download the electronic versions or buy cheaper ones online."

"I wouldn't think that people wanted children's books in digital."

"You'd be surprised. There are some interactive Dr. Seuss books—they're actually quite good. But I'm not sure about the read-to-yourself functions. I think it's still important for parents to read to their kids."

Tess blushed guiltily. She did have *Hop on Pop* on her iPad, along with several games, although Carla Scout so far seemed to prefer opening—and then deleting—her mother's e-mail.

"Anyway," Mona continued, "it's the sudden shrinkage that's making her cranky. Because it's the most expensive, most beautiful books. *Hugo*, things like that. A lot of the Caldecott books, but never the Newberys, and we keep them in the same section. Someone's clearly targeting the illustrated books. Yet not the truly rare ones, which are kept under lock-and-key." She indicated the case that ran along the front of the counter, filled with old books in mint condition: *Elouise Goes to Moscow*, various Maurice Sendak titles, *Emily of Deep Valley*, Eleanor Estes's *100 Dresses*, a book unknown to Tess, *Epaminondas and His Auntie*, whose cover illustration was deeply un-PC.

Tess found herself switching personas, from harried mom to a professional private investigator who provided security consultations. She studied her surroundings. "All these little rooms—it's cozy, but a shoplifter's paradise. An alarm, and a bell on the door to alert you to the door's movement, but no cameras. Have you thought about making people check totes and knapsacks?"

"We tried, but Octavia got the numbers confused and when she gets harried—let's just say, it doesn't bring out her best."

"Octavia?"

"The owner."

As if her name conjured her up, she appeared just like that, slamming back through the door, coffee in hand. "I always forget that the bank closes at three every day but Friday. Oh well. It's not like I had that much to deposit."

She glanced at Mona, her face softer, kinder. She was younger than Tess had realized, not even forty. It was her stern manner and dyed black hair that aged her. "I can write you a check today, but if you could wait until Friday . . ."

"Sure, Octavia. And it's almost Halloween. People will be doing holiday shopping before you know it."

Octavia sighed. "More people in the store.

More distractions. More opportunity." She glanced at Carla Scout, who was sitting on the floor with a Mo Willems book, "reading" it to herself. Tess thought Octavia would have to be charmed in spite of herself. What could be more adorable than a little girl reading, especially this little girl, who had the good sense to favor her father, with fair skin and thick dark hair that was already down to her shoulders. Plus, she was wearing a miniature leather bomber jacket from the Gap, red jeans and a Clash T-shirt. Tess had heard "She's so adorable" at least forty times today. She waited for the forty-first such pronouncement.

Octavia said: "She got chocolate on the book."

So she had. And they already owned *Don't Let the Pigeon Drive the Bus*, but Tess would just have to eat this damaged copy. "I'll add it to my other purchases when I check out," Tess said, knowing it was folly to try to separate Carla Scout from any object that was keeping her quiet and contented.

"I understand you've been having some problems with theft?"

"Mona!" Owner glared at employee. Tess

would have cowered under such a glance, but the younger woman shrugged it off.

"It's not shameful, Octavia. People don't steal from us because we're bad people. Or even because we're bad at what we do. They do it because they're opportunistic."

"A camera would go far in solving your problems," Tess offered.

Octavia sniffed. "I don't do gadgets." She shot another baleful look at Tess's iPad, then added, with slightly less edge: "Besides, I can't afford the outlay just now."

Her honesty softened Tess. "Understood. Have you noticed a pattern?"

"It's not like I can do inventory every week," Octavia began, even as Mona said: "It's Saturdays. I'm almost certain it's Saturdays. It gets busy here, what with the story time and more browsers than usual—often divorced dads, picking up a last-minute gift or just trying desperately to entertain their kids."

"I might be able to help—"

Octavia held up a hand: "I don't have money for that, either."

"I'd do it for free," Tess said, surprising herself.

"Why?" Octavia's voice was edged with

suspicion. She wasn't used to kindness, Tess realized, except, perhaps, from Mona, the kind of employee who would sit on a check for a few days.

"Because I think your store is good for North Baltimore and I want my daughter to grow up coming here. To be a true city kid, to ride her bike or take the bus here, pick out books on her own. *Betsy-Tacy, Mrs. Piggle-Wiggle, The Witch of Blackbird Pond.* Edward Eager and E. Nesbit. All the books I loved."

"Everyone wants to pass their childhood favorites on to their children," Octavia said. "But if I've learned anything in this business, it's that kids have to make their own discoveries if you want them to be true readers."

"Okay, fine. But if I want her to discover books, there's nothing like browsing in a store or a library. There are moments of serendipity that you can't equal." She turned to her daughter just in time to see—but not stop—Carla Scout reaching for another book with her dirty hands. "We'll take that one, too."

Back on Twenty-Fifth Street, Carla Scout strapped in her stroller, Tess was trying to steer with one hand while she held her phone with another, checking e-mails. Inevitably, she ran up on the heels of a man well-known to her, at least by sight.

She and Crow, Carla Scout's father, called him the Walking Man and often wondered about his life, why he had the time and means to walk miles across North Baltimore every day, in every kind of weather, as if on some kind of mission. He might have been handsome if he smiled and stood up straight, but he never smiled and there was a curve to his body that suggested he couldn't stand up straight. When Tess bumped him, he swung sharply away from her, catching Tess with the knapsack he always wore and it was like being hit with a rock. Tess wondered if he weighed it down to help correct his unfortunate posture.

"Sorry," Tess said, but the walking man didn't even acknowledge their collision. He just kept walking with his distinctive, flat-footed style, his body curving forward like a C. There was no bounce, no spring, in Walking Man's stride, only a grim need to put one foot in front of the other, over and over again. He was, Tess thought, like someone under a curse in a fairy tale or myth, sentenced to walk until a spell was broken.

Before her first Saturday shift at the bookstore, Tess consulted her aunt, figuring that she must also see a lot of "shrinkage" at her store.

"Not really," Kitty said. "Books are hard to shoplift, harder to resell. It happens, of course, but I've never seen a systemic ongoing plan, with certain books targeted the way you're describing. This sounds almost like a vendetta against the owner."

Tess thought about Octavia's brusque ways, Mona's stories about how cranky she could get. Still, it was hard to imagine a disgruntled customer going to these lengths. Most people would satisfy themselves by writing a mean review on Yelp.

"I will tell you this," Kitty said. "Years ago—and it was on Twenty-Fifth Street, when it had even more used bookstores—there was a rash of thefts. The owners couldn't believe how much inventory they were losing, and how random it was. But then it stopped, just like that."

"What happened then? I mean, why did it stop? Did they arrest someone?"

"Not to my knowledge."

"I should probably check with the other sellers on the street, see if they're noticing anything," Tess said. "But I wonder why it's happening *now.*"

"Maybe someone's worried that there won't be books much longer, that they're going to be extinct."

It was clearly a joke on Kitty's part, but Tess couldn't help asking: "Are they?"

The pause on the other end of the phone line was so long that Tess began to wonder if her cell had dropped the call. When Kitty spoke again, her voice was low, without its usual mirth.

"I don't dare predict the future. After all, I didn't think newspapers could go away. Still, I believe that there will be a market for physical books; I just don't know how large it will be. All I know is that I'm okay—for now. I own my building, I have a strong core of loyal customers, and I have a good walk-in trade from tourists. In the end, it comes down to what people value. Do they value bookstores? Do they value books? I don't know, Tess.

Books have been free in libraries for years and that didn't devalue them. The Book Thing here in Baltimore gives books away to anyone who wants them. Free, no strings. Doesn't hurt me at all. For decades, people have bought used books from everywhere-from flea markets to the Smith College Book Sale. But there's something about pressing a button on your computer and buying something so ephemeral for 99 cents, having it whooshed instantly to you. Remember *Charlie and the Chocolate Factory?*"

"Of course." Tess, like most children, had been drawn to Roald Dahl's dark stories. He was another one on her list of writers she wanted Carla Scout to read.

"Well, what if you could do what Willie Wonka did—as Dahl fantasized—reach into your television and pull out a candy bar? What if everything you wanted was always available to you, all the time, on a 24/7 basis? It damn near is. Life has become so a la carte. We get what we want when we want it. But if you ask me, that means it's that much harder to identify what we really want."

"That's not a problem in Baltimore," Tess said. "All I can get delivered is pizza and Chinese—and not even my favorite pizza or Chinese."

"You're joking to get me off this morbid school of thought."

"Not exactly." She wasn't joking. The state of food delivery in Baltimore was depressing. But she also wasn't used to hearing her ebullient aunt in such a somber mood and she was trying to distract her, as she might play switcheroo with Carla Scout. And it worked. It turned out that dealing with a toddler, day in and day out, was actually good practice for dealing with the world at large.

The Children's Bookstore was hectic on Saturdays as promised, although Tess quickly realized that there was a disproportionate relationship between the bustle in the aisles and the activity at the cash register.

She also noticed the phenomenon that Mona had described, people using the store as a real-life shopping center for their virtual needs. She couldn't decide which was more obnoxious—the people who pulled out their various devices and made purchases while standing in the store, or those who waited until they were on the sidewalk again, who hunched over their phones and eReaders almost furtively as if committing a kind of crime. They were and they weren't, Tess decided. It was legal, but they were ripping off Mona's space and time, using her as a curator of sorts.

At the height of the hubbub, a delivery man arrived with boxes of books, wheeling his hand truck through the narrow aisles, losing the top box at one point. He was exceedingly handsome in a preppy way—and exceedingly clumsy. As he tried to work his way to the back of the store, his boxes fell off one, two, three times. Once, the top box burst open, spilling a few books onto the floor.

"Sorry," he said with a bright smile as he knelt to collect them. Except—did Tess see him sweep several books off a shelf and into a box? Why would he do that? After all, the boxes were being delivered; it's not as if he could take them with him.

"Tate is the clumsiest guy in the world," Mona said with affection after he left. "A sweetheart, but just a mess."

"You mean, he drops stuff all the time?"

"Drops things, mixes up orders, you name it. But Octavia dotes on him. Those dimples . . . "

Tess had not picked up on the dimples, but she had a chance to see how they affected Octavia when the delivery man returned fifteen minutes later, looking sheepish.

"Tate!" Octavia said with genuine delight.

"I feel so stupid. One of those boxes I left—it's for Royal Books up the block."

"No problem," Octavia said. "You know I never get around to unpacking the Saturday deliveries until the store clears out late in the day."

He looked through the stack of boxes he had left, showed Octavia that one was addressed to Royal Books and hoisted it on his shoulder. Tess couldn't help noticing that there wasn't any tape on the box; the top had been folded with the overlapping flaps that people used when boxing their own possessions for a move. She ambled out in the street behind him, saw him put the box on his truck—then drive away, west and then north on Howard Street, completely bypassing Royal Books.

He looks like someone, Tess thought. *Some-*

one I know, yet don't know. Someone famous? He probably just resembled some actor on television.

Back inside the bookstore, she didn't have the heart to tell Octavia what she suspected. Octavia had practically glowed when she saw Tate. Besides, Tess had no proof. Yet.

"So, did you see anything?" Octavia asked at day's end.

"Maybe. If there was anything taken today, it was from this shelf." Tess pointed to the low one next to where the box had fallen, spilling its contents. Mona crouched on her haunches and poked at the titles. "I can't be sure until I check our computer, but the shelf was full yesterday. I mean—there's no Seuss and we always have Seuss."

"If you saw it, why didn't you say something?" Octavia demanded, as peevish as any paying customer. "Or *do* something, for God's sake."

"I wasn't sure I saw anything and I didn't want to offend . . . a potential customer. I'll be back next Saturday. This is a two-person job." Life is unfair. Tess Monaghan, toting her toddler daughter in a baby carrier, was invisible to most of the world, except for leering men who observed the baby's chest-level position and said things like "Best seat in the house."

But when Crow put on the Ergo and shouldered their baby to *his* chest, the world melted, or at least the female half did. So he stood in the bookstore the next Saturday morning, trying to be polite to the cooing women around him, even as he waited to see if he would observe something similar to what Tess had seen the week before. Once again, Tate arrived when story hour was in full swing, six boxes on his hand truck.

No dropped box, Crow reported via text.

Damn, Tess thought. Maybe he was smart enough to vary the days, despite Mona's conviction that the thefts had been concentrated on Saturdays. Maybe she was deluded, maybe —

Her phone pinged again. *Taking one box with him. Says it was on cart by mistake. I didn't see anything, tho. He's good.*

Tess was on her bike, which she had decided was her best bet for following someone in North Baltimore on a Saturday. A delivery guy, even an off-brand one working the weekends, had to make frequent stops, right? She counted on being able to keep up with him.

And she did, as he moved through his route, although she almost ran down Walking Man near the Baltimore Museum of Art. Still, she was flying along, watching him unload boxes at stop after stop until she realized the flaw in her plan: How could she know which box was the box from the Children's Bookstore?

She sighed, resigned to donating yet another Saturday to The Children's Bookstore.

And another and another and another. The next four Saturdays went by without any incidents. Tate showed up, delivered his boxes, made no mistakes, dropped nothing. Yet, throughout the week, customer requests would point out missing volumes—books listed as in-stock in the computer, yet nowhere to be found in the store.

By the fifth Saturday, the Christmas rush appeared to be on and the store was even more chaotic when Tate arrived—and dropped a box in one of the store's remote corners, one that could never be seen from the cash register or the story-time alcove on the converted sun porch. Tess, out on the street on her bike, ready to ride, watched it unfold via Facetime on Crow's phone, which he was holding at hip level. The action suddenly blurred—Mona, taken into Tess's confidence, had rushed forward try and help Tate. Tate brushed her away, but not before Carla Scout's sippee cup somehow fell on the box, the lid bouncing off and releasing a torrent of red juice, enough to leave a visible splotch on the box's side, an image that Crow captured and forwarded in a text. Tess, across the street, watched as he loaded it, noted the placement of the large stain.

It was a long, cold afternoon, with no respite for Tess as she followed the truck. No time to grab so much as a cup of coffee, and she wouldn't have risked drinking anything because that could have forced her to search out a bathroom.

It was coming up on four o'clock, the wintry light beginning to weaken, when Tate headed up one of the most notorious hills in the residential neighborhood of Roland Park, not far from where Tess lived. She would have loved to wait at the bottom, but how could she know where he made the delivery? She gave him a five-minute head start, hoping that Tate, like most Baltimore drivers, simply didn't see cyclists.

His truck was parked outside a rambling Victorian, perhaps one of the old summer houses built when people would travel a mere five to fifteen miles to escape the closed-in heat of downtown Baltimore. Yet this house, on a street full of million-dollar houses, did not appear to be holding its end up. Cedar shingles had dropped off as if the house were molting, the roof was inexpertly patched in places, and the chimney looked like a liability suit waiting to happen. The delivery truck idled in the driveway, Tate still in the driver's seat. Tess crouched by her wheel in a driveway three houses down, pretending to be engaged in a repair. Eventually, a man came out, but not from the house. He had been inside the stable at the head of the driveway. Most such outbuildings in the neighborhood had been converted to new uses or torn down, but this one appeared to have been untouched. A light burned inside, but that was all Tess could glimpse before the doors rolled shut again.

That man looks familiar, she thought, as she had thought about Tate the first time she saw him. *Is he famous or do I know him?*

The man who walked to the end of the

driveway, she realized, was Walking Man. No backpack, but it was clearly him, his shoulders rounding even farther forward without their usual counterweight. He shook the driver's hand and Tess realized why she thought she had seen Tate before—he was a handsomer, younger version of Walking Man.

Tate handed Walking Man the box with the red stain. No money changed hands. Nothing changed hands. But even in the dim light, the stain was evident. The man took the box into the old stable and muscled the doors back into place.

Tess was faced with a choice, one she hadn't anticipated. She could follow Tate and confront him, figuring that he had the most to lose. His job was on the line. But she couldn't prove he was guilty of theft until she looked inside the box. If she followed Tate, the books could be gone before she returned and she wouldn't be able to prove anything. She had to see what was inside that box.

She texted Crow, told him what she was going to do and walked up the driveway without waiting for his reply, which she supposed would urge caution, or tell her to call the police. But it was only a box of books from a children's bookstore. How high could the stakes be?

She knocked on the stable door. Minutes passed. She knocked again.

"I saw you," she said to the dusk, to herself, possibly to the man inside. "I know you're in there."

Another minute or so passed, a very long time to stand outside as darkness encroached and the cold deepened. But, eventually, the door was rolled open.

"I don't know you," Walking Man said in the flat affect of a child.

"My name is Tess Monaghan and I sort of know you. You're the—"

She stopped herself just in time. Walking Man didn't know he was Walking Man. She realized, somewhat belatedly, that *he* had not boiled his existence down to one quirk. Whoever he was, he didn't define himself as Walking Man. He had a life, a history. Perhaps a sad and gloomy one, based on these surroundings and his compulsive, constant hiking, but he was not, in his head or mirror, a man who did nothing but walk around North Baltimore.

Or was he?

"I've seen you around. I don't live far from here. We're practically neighbors."

He stared at her oddly, said nothing. His arm was braced against the frame of the door—she could not enter without pushing past him. She sensed he wouldn't like that kind of contact, that he was not used to being touched. She remembered how quickly he had whirled around the day she rolled her stroller up on his heels. But unlike most people, who would turn toward the person who had jostled them, he moved away.

"May I come in?"

He dropped his arm and she took that as an invitation—and also as a sign that he believed himself to have nothing to fear. He wasn't acting like someone who felt guilty, or in the wrong. Then again, he didn't know that she had followed the books here.

The juice-stained box sat on a work table, illuminated by an overhead light strung from the ceiling on a long cable. Tess walked over to the box, careful not to turn her back to Walking Man, wishing she had a name for him other than Walking Man, but he had not offered his name when she gave hers.

"May I?" she said, indicating the box, picking up a box cutter next to it, but only because she didn't want him to be able to pick it up.

"It's mine," he said.

She looked at the label. The address was for this house. Cover, should the ruse be discovered? "William Kemper. Is that you?"

"Yes." His manner was odd, off. Then again, she was the one who had shown up at his home and demanded to inspect a box addressed to him. Perhaps he thought she was just another quirky Baltimorean. Perhaps he had a reductive name for her, too. Nosy Woman.

"Why don't you open it?"

He stepped forward and did. There were at least a dozen books, all picture books, all clearly new. He inspected them carefully.

"These are pretty good," he said.

"Good for what?"

He looked at her as if she were quite daft. "My work."

"What do you do?"

"Create."

"The man who brought you the books . . ."

"My younger brother, Tate. He brings me books. He says he knows a place that gives them away free."

"These look brand-new."

He shrugged, uninterested in the observation.

Tess tried again. "Why does your brother bring you books?"

"He said it was better for him to bring them, than for me to get them myself."

Tess again remembered bumping into Walking Man on Twenty-Fifth Street, the hard thwack of his knapsack, so solid it almost left a bruise.

"But you still sometimes get them for yourself, don't you?"

It took him a while to formulate a reply. A dishonest person would have been thinking up a lie all along. An average person would have been considering the pros and cons of lying. William Kemper was just very deliberate with his words.

"Sometimes. Only when they need me."

"Books need you?"

"Books need to breathe after a while. They wait so long. They wait and they wait, closed in. You can tell that no one has read them in a very long time. Or even opened them."

"So you 'liberate' them? Is that your work?"

Walking Man—William—turned away from her and began sorting through the books his brother had brought. He was through with her, or wanted to be.

"These books weren't being neglected. Or ignored."

"No, but they're the only kind of books that Tate knows how to get. He thinks it's all about pictures. I don't want to tell them they're not quite right. I make do with what he brings, and supplement when I have to." He sighed, the sigh of an older brother used to a sibling's screw-ups. Tess had to think that Tate had done his share of sighing, too

"William—were you away for a while?"

"Yes," he said, flipping the pages, studying the pictures, his mind not really on her or their conversation.

"Did you go to prison?"

"They said it wasn't." Flip, flip, flip. "At any rate, I got to come home. Eventually."

"When?"

"Two winters ago." It seemed an odd way to phrase it, pseudo-Native American stuff, affected. But for a walking man, the seasons probably mattered more.

"And this is your house?"

"Mine and Tate's. As long as we can pay the taxes. Which is about all we can do. Pay the taxes."

Tess didn't doubt that. Even a ramshackle pile in this neighborhood would have a tax bill of at least $15,000, maybe $20,000 per year. But did he actually live in the house? Her eyes now accustomed to the gloom, she realized the stable had been converted to an apartment of sorts. There was a cot, a makeshift kitchen with a hot plate, a mini fridge, a radio. A bathroom wasn't evident, but William's appearance would indicate that he had a way to keep himself and his clothes clean.

Then she noticed what was missing: *Books.* Except for the ones that had just arrived, there were no books in evidence.

"Where are the books, William?"

"There," he said, after a moment of confusion. Whatever his official condition, he was very literal.

"No, I mean the others. There are others, right?"

"In the house."

"May I see them?"

"It's almost dark."

"So?"

"That means turning on the lights."

"Doesn't the house have lights?"

"We have an account. Tate said we should keep the utilities, because otherwise the neighbors will complain, say it's dangerous. Water, gas and electric. But we don't use them, except for the washer-dryer and for showers. If it gets really cold, I can stay in the house, but even with the heat on, it's still cold. It's so big. The main thing is to keep it nice enough so no one can complain."

He looked exhausted from such a relatively long speech. Tess could tell that her mere presence was stressful to him. But it didn't seem to be the stress of *discovery*. He wasn't fearful. Other people made him anxious in general. Perhaps that was another reason that Walking Man kept walking. No one could catch up to him and start a conversation.

"I'd like to see the books, William."

"Why?"

"Because I—represent some of the people who used to own them."

"They didn't love them."

"Perhaps." There didn't seem to be any point in arguing with William. "I'd like to see them."

From the outside, Tess had not appreciated how large the house was, how deep into the lot it was built. Even by the standards of the neighborhood, it was enormous, taking up almost every inch of level land on the lot. There was more land still, but it was a long, precipitous slope. They were high here, with a commanding view of the city and the nearby highway. William took her through the rear door, which led into an ordinary, somewhat old-fashioned laundry room with appliances that appeared to be at least ten to fifteen years old.

"The neighbors might call the police," William said, his tone fretful. "Just seeing a light."

"Because they think the house is vacant?"

"Because they would do anything to get us out. Any excuse to call attention to us. Tate says it's important not to let them do that."

He led her through the kitchen, the lights still off. Again, out-of-date, but ordinary and clean, if a bit dusty from disuse. Now they were in a long shadowy hall closed off by French doors, which led to a huge room. William opened these and they entered a multi-windowed room, still dark, but not as dark as the hallway.

"The ballroom. Although we never had any balls that I know of," he said.

A ballroom. This was truly one of the grand old mansions of Roland Park.

"But where are the books, William?" Tess asked.

He blinked, surprised. "Oh, I guess you need more light. I thought the lights from the other houses would be enough." He flipped a switch and the light from overhead chandeliers filled the room. Yet the room was quite empty.

"The books, William. Where are they?"

"All around you."

And it was only then that Tess realized that what appeared to be an unusual, slapdash wallpaper was made from pages—pages and pages and pages of books. Some were only text, but at some point during the massive project—the ceilings had to be at least 20, possibly 30 feet high—the children's books began to appear. Tess stepped closer to inspect what he had done. She didn't have a craft-y bone in her body, but it appeared to be similar to some kind of decoupage—there was definitely a sealant over the pages. But it wasn't UV protected because there were sun streaks on the wall that faced south and caught the most light.

She looked down and realized he had done the same thing with the floor, or started to; part of the original parquet floor was still in evidence.

"Is the whole house like this?"

"Not yet," he said. "It's a big house."

"But William—these books, they're not yours. You've destroyed them."

"How?" he said. "You can still read them. The pages are in order. I'm letting them live. They were dying, inside their covers, on shelves. No one was looking at them. Now they're open forever, always ready to be read."

"But no one can see them here either," she said.

"I can. You can."

"William is my half-brother," Tate Kemper told Tess a few days later, over lunch in the Paper Moon Diner, a North Baltimore spot that was a kind of shrine to old toys. "He's fifteen years older than I am. He was institutionalized for a while. Then our grandfather, our father's father, agreed to pay for his care, set him up with an aide, in a little apartment not far from here. He left us the house in his will and his third wife got everything else. My mom and I never had money, so it's not a big deal to me. But our dad was still rich when William was young, so no one worried about how he would take care of himself when he was an adult."

"If you sold the house, you could easily pay for William's care, at least for a time."

"Yes, even in a bad market, even with the antiquated systems and old appliances, it probably would go for almost a million. But William begged me to keep it, to let him try living alone. He said grandfather was the only person who was ever nice to him and he was right. His mother is dead and our father is a shit, gone from both of our lives, disinherited by his own father. So I let William move into the stable. It was several months before I realized what he was doing."

"But he'd done it before, no?"

Tate nodded. "Yes, he was caught stealing books years ago. Several times. We began to worry he was going to run afoul of some repeat offenders law, so grandfather offered to pay for psychiatric care as part of a plea bargain. Then, when he got out, the aide watched him, kept him out of trouble. But once he had access to grandfather's house . . ." He shook his head, sighing in the same way William had sighed.

"How many books have you stolen for him?"

"Fifty, a hundred. I tried to spread it out to several places, but the other owners are, well, a little sharper than Octavia."

No, they're just not smitten with you, Tess wanted to say.

"Could you make restitution?"

"Over time. But what good would it do? William will just steal more. I'm stuck. Besides . . ." Tate looked defiant, proud. "I think what he's doing is kind of beautiful."

Tess didn't disagree. "The thing is, if something happens to you—if you get caught, or lose your job—you're both screwed. You can't go on like this. And you have to make restitution to Octavia. Do it anonymously, through me, whatever you can afford. Then I'll show you how William can get all the books he needs, for free."

"I don't see—"

"Trust me," Tess said. "And one other thing?"

34

"Sure."

"Would it kill you to ask Octavia out for coffee or something? Just once?"

"Octavia! If I were going to ask someone there out, it would be—"

"Mona, I know. But you know what, Tate? Not everyone can get the girl with the duck tattoo."

The next Saturday, Tess met William outside his house. He wore his knapsack on his back, she wore hers on the front, where Carla Scout nestled with a sippee cup. She was small for her age, not even twenty-five pounds, but it was still quite the cargo to carry on a hike.

"Are you ready for our walk?"

"I usually walk alone," William said. He was unhappy with this arrangement and had agreed to it only after Tate had all but ordered him to do it.

"After today, you can go back to walking alone. But I want to take you some place today. It's almost three miles."

"That's nothing," William said.

"Your pack might be heavier on the return trip."

"It often is," he said.

I bet, Tess thought. He had probably never given up stealing books despite what Tate thought.

They walked south through the neighborhood, lovely even with the trees bare and the sky overcast. William, to Tess's surprise, preferred the main thoroughfares. Given his aversion to people, she thought he would want to duck down less-trafficked side streets, make use of Stony Run Park's green expanse, which ran parallel to much of their route. But William stuck to the busiest streets. She wondered if drivers glanced out their windows and thought: Oh, the walking man now has a walking woman and a walking baby.

He did not speak and shut down any attempt Tess made at conversation. He walked as if he were alone. His face was set, his gait steady. She could tell it made him anxious, having to follow her path, so she began to narrate the route, turn by turn, which let him walk a few steps ahead. "We'll take Roland Avenue to University Parkway, all the way to Barclay, where we'll go left." His pace was slow by Tess's standards, but William didn't walk to get places. He walked to walk. He walked to fill his days. Tate said his official diagnosis was bi-polar with OCD, which made finding the right mix of medications difficult. His work, as William termed it, seemed to keep him more grounded than anything else, which was why Tate indulged it.

Finally, about an hour later, they stood outside a building of blue-and-pink cinderblocks.

"This is it," Tess said.

"This is what?"

"Go in."

They entered a warehouse stuffed with books. And not just any books—these were all unloved books, as William would have it, books donated to this unique Baltimore institution, the Book Thing, which accepted any and all books on one condition: They would then be offered free to anyone who wanted them.

"Tens of thousands of books," Tess said. "All free, every weekend."

"Is there a limit?"

"Yes," Tess said. "Only ten at a time. But you probably couldn't carry much more, right?" Actually, the limit, according to the Book Thing's rather whimsical website, was 150,000. But Tess had decided her aunt was right about people according more value to things they could not have so readily. If William thought he could have only ten, every week, it would be more meaningful to him.

He walked through the aisles, his eyes strafing the spines. "How will I save them all?" William said.

"One week at a time," Tess said. "But you have to promise that this will be your only, um, supplier from now on. If you get books from anywhere else, you won't be allowed to come here anymore. Do you understand, William? Can you agree to that?"

"I'll manage," William said. "These books really need me."

It took him forty-five minutes to pick his first book, *Manifold Destiny*, a guide to cooking on one's car engine.

"Really?" Tess said. "That's a book that needs to be liberated?"

William looked at her with pity, as if she were a hopeless philistine.

"He spent five hours there, selecting his books," Tess told Crow that evening, over an early supper. Crow worked Saturday evenings, so they ate early in order to spend more time together.

"Did you feel guilty at all? He's just going to tear them apart and destroy them."

"Is he? Destroying them, I mean. Or is he making something beautiful, as his brother would have it? I go back and forth."

Crow shook his head. "An emotionally disturbed man with scissors, cutting up books inside his home, taking a walk with you and our daughter, whose middle name is Scout. And you didn't make one Boo Radley joke the entire time?"

"Not a one," Tess said. "You do the bath. I'll clean up."

But she didn't clean up, not right away. She went into her own library, a cozy sunroom lined with bookshelves. She had spent much of her pregnancy here, reading away, but even in three months of confinement she barely made a dent in the unread books. She had always thought of it as being rich, having so many books she had yet to read. But in William's view, she was keeping them confined. And no one else, other than Crow, had access to them. Was her library that different from William's?

Of course, she had paid for her books— most of them. Like almost every other bibliophile on the planet, Tess had books, borrowed from friends, that she had never returned, even as some of her favorite titles lingered in friends' homes, never to be seen again.

She picked up her iPad. Only seventy books loaded onto it. *Only.* Mainly things for work, but also the occasional self-help guide that promised to unlock the mysteries of toddlers. Forty of the seventy titles were virtually untouched. She wandered into Carla Scout's room, where there was now a poster of a bearded man living in a pile of books, the Arnold Lobel print from The Children's Bookstore. A payment/gift from a giddy Octavia, who didn't know how Tess had stopped her books from disappearing, and certainly didn't know that her crush had anything to do with it. During Carla Scout's bedtime routine, Tess now stopped in front of the poster, read the verse printed there, then added her own couplet. "It's just as much fun as it looks/To live in a house made of books."

It's what's in the book that matters. Standing in her daughter's room, which also had shelves and shelves filled with books, Tess remembered a character in a favorite story saying that to someone who objected to using the Bible as a fan on a hot summer day. But she could no longer remember which story it was.

Did that mean the book had ceased to live for her? The title she was trying to recall could be in this very room, along with all of Tess's childhood favorites, waiting for Carla Scout to discover them one day. But what if she rejected them all, insisting on her own myths and legends, as Octavia had prophesied? How many of these books would be out of print in five, ten years? What did it mean to be out of print in a world where books could live inside devices, glowing like captured genies, desperate to get back out in the world and grant people's wishes?

Carla Scout burst into the room, wet hair gleaming, cheeks pink.

"Buh," she said, which was her word for book, unless it was her word for ball or, possibly, balloon. "Buh, p'ease."

She wasn't even in her pajamas yet, just her diaper and hooded towel. Tess would have to use the promise of books to coax her through putting on her footed sleeper and gathering up her playthings. How long would she be able to bribe her daughter with books? Would they be shunted aside like the Velveteen Rabbit as other newer, shinier toys gained favor? Would her daughter even read *The Velveteen Rabbit?* William Kemper suddenly seemed less crazy to Tess than the people who managed to live their lives in houses that had no books at all.

"Three tonight," Tess said. "Pick out three. Only three, Carla Scout. One, two, three. You may have three."

They read five.

Author's note: The Book Thing is a very real thing and its hours and policies are as described here. The Children's Bookstore on 25th Street is my invention, along with all characters.